This book belongs to

_____

A READ-ALOUD STORYBOOK

ADAPTED BY
Lisa Marsoli

ILLUSTRATED BY
Elizabeth Tate, Caroline LaVelle Egan, Studio IBOIX,
Michael Inman, and Jean-Paul Orpiñas

DESIGNED BY
Deborah Boone

Random House 🏠 New York

Copyright © 2009 Disney Enterprises, Inc. All rights reserved. The movie THE PRINCESS AND THE FROG Copyright © 2009 Disney, story inspired in part by the book THE FROG PRINCESS by E.D. Baker Copyright © 2002, published by Bloomsbury Publishing, Inc. Published in the United States by Random House Children's Books, a division of Random House, Inc., 1745 Broadway, New York, NY 10019, and in Canada by Random House of Canada Limited, Toronto, in conjunction with Disney Enterprises, Inc. Random House and the colophon are registered trademarks of Random House, Inc.

Library of Congress Control Number: 2009007485

ISBN: 978-0-7364-2573-5

www.randomhouse.com/kids

Printed in the United States of America

10 9 8

One evening, little Tiana was sitting in the New Orleans mansion of her friend Charlotte LaBouff. Tiana's mother, Eudora, sewed a beautiful dress as she read a story about a frog who needed a kiss to turn him into a human prince.

"There is no way in this whole wide world I would ever kiss a frog!" Tiana exclaimed.

But Charlotte said, "I would kiss a hundred frogs if I could marry a prince and be a princess."

Back at home, Tiana happily finished cooking dinner with her father, James. They dreamed of opening their own restaurant together someday.

"This is the best gumbo I've ever tasted!" he declared. "A gift this special just has to be shared!"

Soon the whole neighborhood gathered around their porch to enjoy the good food.

Later, as Tiana nestled into bed, James encouraged his daughter to make a wish on the Evening Star. "And then, if you work hard enough, you can be anything you want," James said. "Just never lose sight of what's really important, okay?"

As soon as her parents left the room, Tiana wished: "Please help us get our restaurant!"

Years went by, and Tiana grew up to be a beautiful young woman. Her father had passed away, but she still dreamed of opening a restaurant. So Tiana waited tables at Duke's Diner day and night and saved every spare penny she could. She knew that her hard work would pay off one day.

Not far away, a prince from a foreign land arrived in town. Unlike Tiana, Prince Naveen was not interested in working at all. He was visiting because he loved jazz music, and New Orleans was filled with jazz, jazz, jazz! Naveen quickly joined in the fun of the big festival called Mardi Gras. His valet, Lawrence, struggled to keep up!

Everyone in town was buzzing about the prince's arrival, but Tiana hardly noticed. She was much too busy even to go dancing with her friends.

"I'm going to work a double shift," Tiana said.

"Girl, all you ever do is work!" exclaimed her friend Georgia.

Just then, Charlotte and her father, Big Daddy LaBouff, came into Duke's Diner.

Charlotte excitedly told Tiana that Prince Naveen was coming to her father's masquerade ball that very night! "I'm going to need about five hundred of your man-catching beignets."

After Charlotte paid her, Tiana finally had enough money for a down payment on her restaurant!

That afternoon, an overjoyed Tiana made an offer on the old
sugar mill. It was the location she and her father had chosen for
their restaurant long ago. With Eudora by her side, Tiana felt as
if her dream was about to come true! The brokers, Mr. Fenner
and his brother, Mr. Fenner, happily accepted the down payment.

"Oh, can't you just picture it, Mama?" Tiana said excitedly, imagining the sugar mill as her restaurant. "It'll be the place Daddy and I always dreamed of."

"Tiana," Eudora replied gently, "your daddy may not have gotten the place he always wanted, but he had something better. He had love. And that's all I want for you, sweetheart."

Meanwhile, a sinister man named Dr. Facilier had lured Prince Naveen and Lawrence into his lair. Dr. Facilier read their tarot cards and promised both men that he could give them exactly what they most desired. Lawrence wanted to be more like the prince instead of carrying his luggage; Naveen wanted to keep up his carefree, happy lifestyle.

As Dr. Facilier held up a magic talisman, Naveen and Lawrence's world began to change. . . .

That evening, Charlotte was delighted when the prince arrived at the masquerade ball! She didn't know that he was actually Lawrence in disguise! Dr. Facilier had used his evil magic to make the switch. The doctor's wicked plan was for Lawrence to marry Charlotte. Then Dr. Facilier and Lawrence would steal all of Big Daddy LaBouff's money.

Charlotte happily danced with the impostor, while Tiana
served beignets to Mr. Fenner and Mr. Fenner.

"You were outbid," the second Mr. Fenner said to a stunned
Tiana. He told her that if she didn't come up with more
money, she would lose the sugar mill! Tiana was heartbroken.

"We had an agreement," she argued, trying to reason with
the men. Unfortunately, she tripped, and toppled onto her
beignet table. Her dress was ruined!

Charlotte took Tiana upstairs to her bedroom and gave her a beautiful princess costume to change into.

"Aren't you just as pretty as a magnolia in May!" Charlotte exclaimed before rushing off.

Alone, Tiana looked up at the Evening Star from the balcony. She really wanted that sugar mill. So she closed her eyes and made a wish. . . .

When Tiana opened her eyes again, she saw a frog.

"A kiss would be nice," the frog said. He was a talking frog! Tiana shrieked and ran back into Charlotte's room as fast as she could.

"I am Prince Naveen of Maldonia," the frog said. He explained that he needed a kiss to become human again. "Surely I could offer you some type of reward. A wish I could grant?"

Tiana wanted to help. And getting her restaurant would be a nice reward, so—SMOOCH! Then . . . POOF! Naveen was still a frog. But Tiana had become a frog, too!

"Aaiieeeeee!" she screamed. "What did you do to me?"

21

In the guest quarters of the LaBouff estate, Dr. Facilier was furious that Naveen had escaped! You see, the doctor needed the prince to make his magic talisman work—and to keep Lawrence looking like Naveen!

"You just win Charlotte's scented hand, and we'll split the big fat fortune," Dr. Facilier angrily told the disguised valet.

Meanwhile, the two new frogs had been chased from the ball into the bayou. That was when Naveen learned that Tiana was not a real princess.

"No wonder the kiss didn't work!" he exclaimed. But Naveen couldn't be too angry. He wasn't really rich and couldn't give Tiana the money for her restaurant. His parents had cut off his allowance until he learned to be more responsible. But there was no time to argue—the two frogs had to figure out how to escape the swamp!

The next morning, Naveen slept while Tiana built a little raft. Later, as Tiana struggled to paddle through the bayou, Naveen lazily strummed a makeshift ukulele. It was clear that she was going to have to do all the work.

Suddenly, an alligator rose to the surface! Luckily, he wasn't hungry—he had come up to hear Naveen's music. The alligator's name was Louis, and he loved jazz and playing his trumpet.

Naveen was happy just to chat and play music with Louis. But Tiana was impatient to find a way to break the spell! Louis told Tiana and Naveen that an old voodoo woman named Mama Odie might be able to help them.

Meanwhile, at the LaBouff estate, Lawrence was proposing to Charlotte. But without the real Naveen, the talisman's magic was wearing off. Luckily, Charlotte was so thrilled that she didn't notice Lawrence changing back into his true self!

"We're going to have ourselves a Mardi Gras wedding!" she squealed. She was going to be a princess!

Back in the bayou, Tiana and Naveen were learning that they couldn't stand each other. They also discovered that being frogs wasn't easy! They hungrily tried to catch a firefly with their sticky tongues—and got tied up in knots instead!

"Let me shine a little light on the situation," the firefly said as he untangled Tiana and Naveen. Then he kindly offered to lead them to Mama Odie.

The helpful firefly's name was Ray. As he traveled along with his new friends, he spoke of his true love, Evangeline. "She is the prettiest firefly that ever did glow."

"Just do not settle down too quickly," Naveen advised Ray.

Frustrated with Naveen's carefree attitude, Tiana hacked through the thick bayou. She just wanted to find Mama Odie and become human again. Then she could be rid of the all-play, no-work prince for good!

Suddenly—*whoosh!*—Naveen was caught in a net! Three
hunters wanted frog legs for dinner.

Ray raced to help his friend. He flew right up the nose of one
of the hunters. Meanwhile, the two other hunters trapped Tiana!

Working together, the two frogs quickly hopped around, causing the hunters to hit each other instead of the frogs!

"Those are the smartest frogs I've seen," one hunter said as all three men lay beaten and battered at the bottom of their boat.

"And we talk, too!" Tiana replied.

Laughing, Tiana and Naveen watched the shocked hunters flee in fear.

After the excitement was over, Tiana started to prepare dinner. Naveen tried to help, but he didn't know how. "The day my parents cut me off, I suddenly realized I didn't know how to do anything."

Tiana began to see the helpless prince in a new light. Gently, she taught him how to chop mushrooms. Soon the gumbo was ready. Ray and Louis loved what Naveen and Tiana had cooked together!

After dinner, Ray gazed up at the sky. "There she is—the sweetest firefly in all creation!" he declared.

Evangeline was the Evening Star!

As Louis began to play his trumpet, Naveen asked Tiana to dance.

Suddenly, evil shadows sent by Dr. Facilier swept into the bayou. They snatched Naveen and began to drag him away. Tiana, Louis, and Ray tried to stop them, but the shadows were too strong!

FOOOOOM! Blinding flashes of light vaporized the wicked shadows one by one. Naveen was saved—but by whom?

"Not bad for a hundred-and-ninety-seven-year-old blind lady," someone said with a laugh. It was Mama Odie!

The magical woman and her pet snake, Juju, led the travelers into her old shrimp-boat home.

"We need to be human," Tiana begged.

"You *want* to be human, but you're blind to what you *need!*" Mama Odie explained. The frogs didn't understand. The old woman sighed and began to stir her gumbo. Tiana peeked into the tub and saw Charlotte becoming the princess of Mardi Gras for the night.

It was suddenly all clear: If Naveen could kiss "Princess" Charlotte before midnight, then he and Tiana would both become human again!

Tiana, Naveen, Louis, and Ray caught a ride on a riverboat to Mardi Gras. Along the way, Naveen confessed to Ray that he had fallen in love with Tiana!

Naveen surprised Tiana with a romantic dinner. But just as he was about to ask her to marry him, Tiana spotted something on the riverbank. "Daddy and I knew that one day that sugar mill would be home to our restaurant," she said dreamily.

Heartbroken, Naveen hopped away. He realized that he could never afford to buy Tiana her restaurant—unless he married Charlotte. But before the frog could ponder this any further, Dr. Facilier's evil shadows captured him!

A little later, at the LaBouff estate, the shadows swept in with Naveen. Dr. Facilier quickly used the prince to restore the talisman's magic. Soon Lawrence would look just like Prince Naveen again and marry Charlotte.

Just when the poor frog finally understood the wicked plot, Dr. Facilier locked him in a chest.

Meanwhile, Ray revealed to Tiana how Naveen really felt: "He's in love with you!"

Tiana was overjoyed. She raced to the parade to see if Naveen had kissed Charlotte yet. Instead, she saw Charlotte and the human Prince Naveen getting married! Not realizing that it was really Lawrence in disguise, Tiana was crushed. She hopped away alone, thinking she would remain a frog forever—and that her dreams would never come true.

Luckily, Ray found the real Naveen and released him from the chest. Together, the two friends tried to stop Charlotte from marrying Lawrence. Just before the couple said "I do," Naveen grabbed the talisman from the impostor's neck and tossed it to Ray.

"Stay out of sight!" Dr. Facilier hissed at Lawrence, who now looked like his old self again.

In a different part of the parade, Louis was having the time of his life, playing his trumpet with a Mardi Gras band. Just then, Ray flew by, struggling with the heavy talisman. Dr. Facilier and the sinister shadows swiftly chased the tired firefly. Jazz would have to wait—Louis's friend needed help! The alligator jumped off the float and followed the action.

Soon Ray found Tiana and gave her the talisman. She ran off with the magical charm. Furious, Dr. Facilier swatted Ray!

As the dark shadows closed in, Dr. Facilier blew a puff of magic dust to create an illusion. Tiana was human again—and in her dream restaurant! "All you have to do to make this a reality is hand over that little ol' charm of mine," Dr. Facilier said.

Suddenly, Tiana understood everything. Her father had been surrounded by love. He'd always had what he needed—and he had never forgotten what was important. She smashed the talisman.

All at once, Tiana was back in reality. And she was a frog again. With the talisman shattered, Dr. Facilier lost his control over the shadows.

Tiana watched in terror as the dark creatures surrounded the evil man. Soon all that was left of Dr. Facilier was his black top hat.

Tiana hopped off to find Naveen. She arrived just in time to hear the prince agree to marry Charlotte.

"But remember," Naveen said to the Mardi Gras princess, "you must give Tiana all the money she requires for her restaurant. Because Tiana? She is my Evangeline."

"Wait!" Tiana called to Naveen. "My dream wouldn't be complete without you in it."

Tears filled Charlotte's eyes. "All my life I read about true love in fairy tales," she said. "Tiana, you found it!" She turned to Naveen. "I'll kiss you, Your Highness. No marriage required!"

But it was too late. The clock chimed midnight. Tiana and Naveen were still frogs, but they were together—and they had found true love.

Suddenly, Louis ran toward them, carrying Ray. The little firefly's light was flickering low. Dr. Facilier had hurt Ray badly.

With tears in their eyes, Naveen and Tiana held hands. "We're staying together," they told him.

"I like that very much," Ray said, smiling. "Evangeline likes that, too." And then the little bug's light went out for the last time.

Later, in the bayou, it was time to bid Ray good-bye forever. All of Ray's friends raised their eyes skyward to gaze at the dazzling Evening Star. Next to it, there was another bright star—a star no one had ever seen before. Ray and Evangeline were together at last.

The little firefly had been right all along. True love always finds a way. . . .

Not long after, Naveen and Tiana were married by Mama Odie. As Naveen kissed Tiana, the two frogs turned back into humans!

"Like I told you, kissing a princess breaks the spell!" Mama Odie said with a laugh.

"And once you became my wife," Naveen began, "that made you—"

"A princess!" Tiana finished. "You just kissed yourself a princess!"

Tiana and Naveen returned to New Orleans, where they had a royal wedding.

Prince Naveen's parents were proud to see their son settle down, and Eudora was thrilled that her daughter had finally found true happiness.

Soon there was a new restaurant in town—
Tiana's Palace. It was the best place to go for good
food, lively music, and fun with friends and family.
Tiana had nothing more to wish for, because
she had everything she'd ever wanted—
and everything she needed.